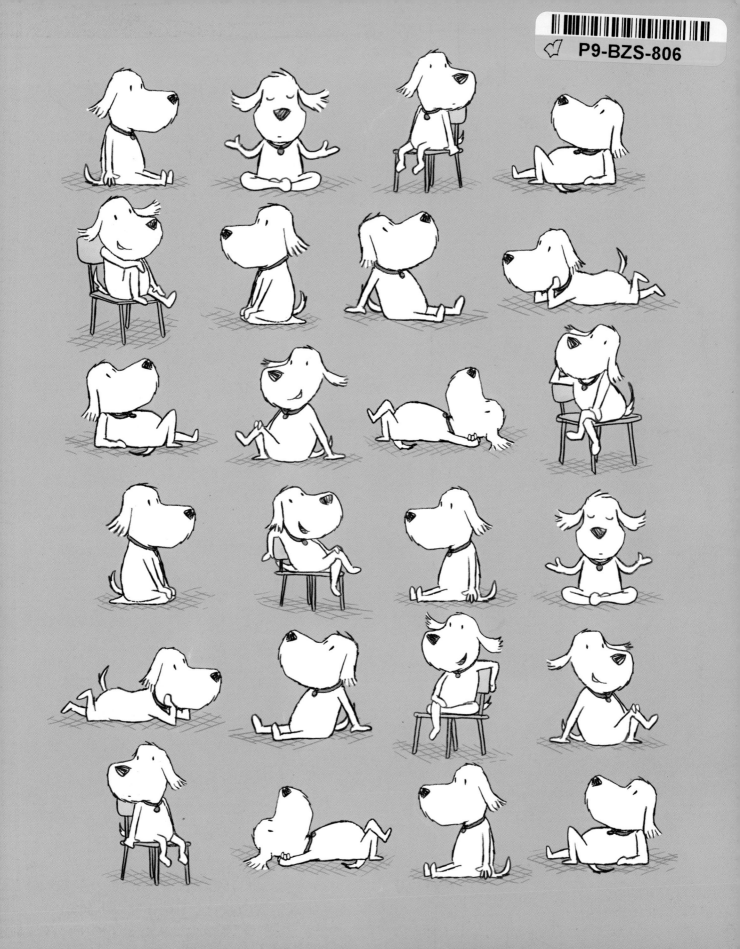

My Dog, Bob

My Dog, Bob

Richard Torrey

Holiday House / New York

This is my dog, Bob.

Like all dogs, Bob loves breakfast.

Sometimes he makes it himself.

And like many dogs, Bob loves
to ride in the car . . .

. . . especially when he's driving.

Most of all, Bob likes to go outside.

He likes to take naps.

And he likes to dig for bones.

My neighbor Mimi has a dog too.
Her name is Truffles.
"My dog is better than your dog,"
Mimi said.

"Truffles can catch a stick," Mimi said.
"Can Bob catch a stick?"

I threw a stick.

But Bob did not catch it.

"Truffles can sit," Mimi said.
"Can Bob sit?"

But Bob did not sit.

"Truffles can speak," Mimi said.
"Can Bob speak?"

But Bob did not speak.

"We win!" said Mimi.

"I'm sorry," said Bob.
"That's okay," I said.

"Let's get something to eat."

To all the Bobs out there—quietly amazing

Copyright © 2015 by Richard Torrey
All Rights Reserved
HOLIDAY HOUSE is registered in the U.S. Patent and Trademark Office.
Printed and Bound in April 2015 at Toppan Leefung, DongGuan City, China.
The artwork was created with watercolor and oil pencil.
www.holidayhouse.com
First Edition
1 3 5 7 9 10 8 6 4 2

Library of Congress Cataloging-in-Publication Data
Torrey, Rich, author, illustrator.
My dog, Bob / Richard Torrey. — First edition.
pages cm
Summary: "Like all dogs, Bob likes breakfast, takes rides in the family car and digs for bones. He's just like any other
dog—except for a few quirks"— Provided by publisher.
ISBN 978-0-8234-3386-5 (hardcover : alk. paper) [1. Dogs—Fiction. 2. Humorous stories.] I. Title.
PZ7.T64573My 2015
[E]—dc23
2014036926

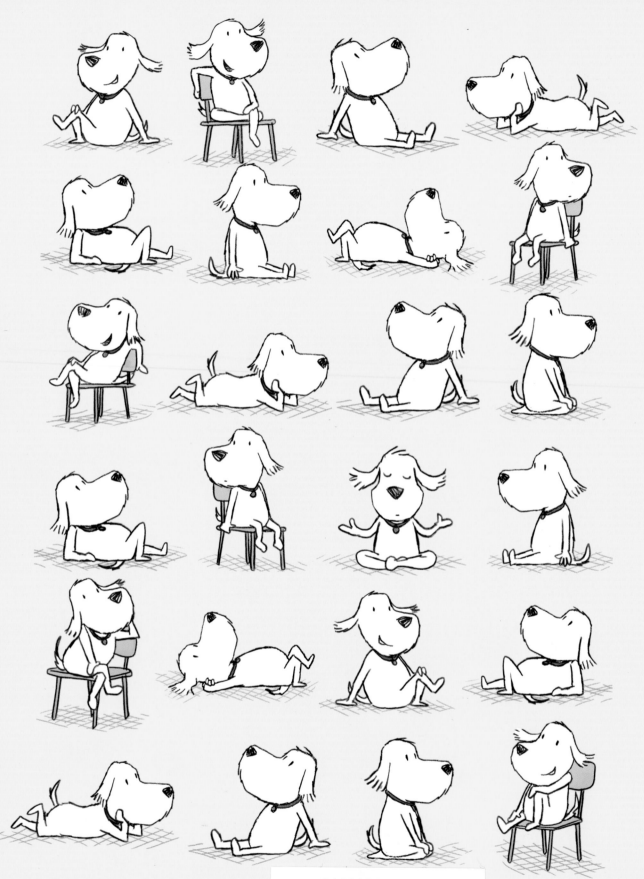